The Eyes Have It

The Eyes Have It
PHILIP K. DICK

ÆGYPAN PRESS

This story from *Science Fiction Stories*, 1953.

Special thanks to Greg Weeks, Barbara Tozier, and the
Online Distributed Proofreading Team (which can be
found at http://www.pgdp.net).

The Eyes Have It
A publication of
ÆGYPAN PRESS

www.aegypan.com

A little whimsy, now and then, makes for good balance. Theoretically, you could find this type of humor anywhere. But only a topflight science-fictionist, we thought, could have written this story, in just this way. . . .

*I*t was quite by accident I discovered this in-credible invasion of Earth by lifeforms from another planet. As yet, I haven't done anything about it; I can't think of anything to do. I wrote to the Government, and they sent back a pam-phlet on the repair and maintenance of frame houses. Anyhow, the whole thing is known; I'm not the first to discover it. Maybe it's even under control.

I was sitting in my easy chair, idly turning the pages of a paperbacked book someone had left on the bus, when I came across the reference that first put me on the trail. For a moment I didn't respond. It took some time for the full import to sink in. After I'd comprehended, it seemed odd I hadn't noticed it right away.

The reference was clearly to a nonhuman species of incredible properties, not indigenous to Earth. A species, I hasten to point out, customarily masquerading as ordinary human beings. Their disguise, however, became transparent in the face of the following observations by the author. It was at once obvious the author knew everything. Knew everything — and was taking it in his stride. The line (and I tremble remembering it even now) read:

. . . his eyes slowly roved about the room.

Vague chills assailed me. I tried to picture the eyes. Did they roll like dimes? The passage indicated not; they seemed to move through the air, not over the surface. Rather rapidly, apparently. No one in the story was surprised. That's what tipped me off. No sign of amazement at such an outrageous thing. Later the matter was amplified.

. . . his eyes moved from person to person.

There it was in a nutshell. The eyes had clearly come apart from the rest of him and were on their own. My heart pounded and my breath choked in my windpipe. I had stumbled on an accidental mention of a totally unfamiliar race. Obviously non-Terrestrial. Yet, to the characters in the book, it was perfectly natural — which suggested they belonged to the same species.

And the author? A slow suspicion burned in my mind. The author was taking it rather *too easily* in his stride. Evidently, he felt this was quite a usual thing. He made absolutely no attempt to conceal this knowledge. The story continued:

. . . presently his eyes fastened on Julia.

Julia, being a lady, had at least the breeding to feel indignant. She is described as blushing and knitting her brows angrily. At this, I sighed with relief. They weren't *all* non-Terrestrials. The narrative continues:

> *. . . slowly, calmly, his eyes examined every inch of her.*

Great Scott! But here the girl turned and stomped off and the matter ended. I lay back in my chair gasping with horror. My wife and family regarded me in wonder.

"What's wrong, dear?" my wife asked.

I couldn't tell her. Knowledge like this was too much for the ordinary run-of-the-mill person. I had to keep it to myself. "Nothing," I gasped. I leaped up, snatched the book, and hurried out of the room.

*I*n the garage, I continued reading. There was more. Trembling, I read the next revealing passage:

> . . . he put his arm around Julia. Presently she asked him if he would remove his arm. He immediately did so, with a smile.

It's not said what was done with the arm after the fellow had removed it. Maybe it was left standing upright in the corner. Maybe it was thrown away. I don't care. In any case, the full meaning was there, staring me right in the face.

Here was a race of creatures capable of removing portions of their anatomy at will. Eyes, arms — and maybe more. Without batting an eyelash. My knowledge of biology came in handy, at this point. Obviously they were simple beings, uni-cellular, some sort of primitive single-celled things. Beings no more developed than starfish. Starfish can do the same thing, you know.

I read on. And came to this incredible revelation, tossed off coolly by the author without the faintest tremor:

> . . . *outside the movie theater we split up. Part of us went inside, part over to the café for dinner.*

Binary fission, obviously. Splitting in half and forming two entities. Probably each lower half went to the café, it being farther, and the upper halves to the movies. I read on, hands shaking. I had really stumbled onto something here. My mind reeled as I made out this passage:

. . . I'm afraid there's no doubt about it. Poor Bibney has lost his head again.

Which was followed by:

. . . and Bob says he has utterly no guts.

Yet Bibney got around as well as the next person. The next person, however, was just as strange. He was soon described as:

. . . totally lacking in brains.

*T*here was no doubt of the thing in the next passage. Julia, whom I had thought to be the one normal person, reveals herself as also being an alien life form, similar to the rest:

> . . . *quite deliberately, Julia had given her heart to the young man.*

It didn't relate what the final disposition of the organ was, but I didn't really care. It was evident Julia had gone right on living in her usual manner, like all the others in the book. Without heart, arms, eyes, brains, viscera, dividing up in two when the occasion demanded. Without a qualm.

. . . thereupon she gave him her hand.

I sickened. The rascal now had her hand, as well as her heart. I shudder to think what he's done with them, by this time.

. . . he took her arm.

Not content to wait, he had to start dismantling her on his own. Flushing crimson, I slammed the book shut and leaped to my feet. But not in time to escape one last reference to those carefree bits of anatomy whose travels had originally thrown me on the track:

. . . her eyes followed him all the way down the road and across the meadow.

I rushed from the garage and back inside the warm house, as if the accursed things were following me. My wife and children were play-ing Monopoly in the kitchen. I joined them and played with frantic fervor, brow feverish, teeth chattering.

I had had enough of the thing. I want to hear no more about it. Let them come on. Let them invade Earth. I don't want to get mixed up in it.

I have absolutely no stomach for it.